This book is dedicated to those who helped me find my twinkle,
my grandchildren : Serenity, Cadence, Presley, Lily,
Payton, Gwenevere, Maddox, Trinity, Josephine,
and my stepgrands : Jade, Emil, and Adriana . . .

and those who may still come.

In addition, a sincere thank you to all my friends and family
for supporting me.

Written by D Bosch
Illustrated by Jeanine-Jonee
Edited by Emily Brigolin

ISBN
978-0-578-95477-6

THE TWINKLE WITCH

There was an old hag, a special ol' biddy,

she had one fine bat and a ferocious sweet kitty.

She had a grand broom and some special friends dear,

and as you can see, she kept them quite near.

Some called her a witch, she was yes, it's true—

and this is a story about her, just for you.

I shall tell you a tale, my fine little ones,

about this old witch and what she had done.

It happened a long, long time ago,

when days became short, and the air became cold.

'Twas the time of harvest, lots of work need be done–

for much had been growing in the warmth of the sun.

But time had come to reap what had grown,

from seeds– months ago, so carefully sown.

The farmers all toiled their days away, yes...

as did the wives and children, no one took rest.

With hearts full of song and eyes full of light,

the reaping got done from daybreak 'til night.

Then harvest came to a halt– it was through–

except one last thing the village would do.

A celebration– a festival grand.

A potluck and bonfire was part of the plan.

To give thanks to the soil for bearing so much,

and to keep away evil that may try to touch

the fertile ground or the children who grow

into the next generation to sow.

As the witch of the town, she'd celebrate too.

Her pot luck item would be Gigglie Stew.

But for that she needed the tears of a bee,

and one piece of bark from a Gigglie Tree.

So with that in mind, she set off on her quest.

In search of items to make her stew the best!

She wandered and searched and looked all around,

surprised she was, when she glanced to the ground.

'Cause there on the street, among gravel and stone,

danced a glimmering shimmering light all alone!

Intrigued she was, at what she saw there—

a shimmering light that bounced everywhere.

And the longer she watched, the more she could see

that the shimmering light was special indeed.

It circled her feet and bounced off her nose,

then tried to tickle her right through her clothes!

Then, she spoke to herself,

"Ye ol' witch, you must, capture this airy bit of bright dust!

To have and to hold – this light must be mine."

So, she planned out a trap for the small bit of shine.

Her quest for the bark of the Gigglie tree

and tears from a bee she no longer did need.

Now she must have this twinkly thing –

a pinch in her stew should give it a zing!

She had a small sweet in the folds of her frock,

that she placed in her palm and she started to talk.

She said...

"Oh, little light that skitters and plays-

would you like to taste my candy today?"

And the light danced a bit, a wee zig and zag,

then landed it did, in the hand of the hag.

She cupped her hands closed-and then, don't ya know,

her eyesight got keen and her senses did grow-

all at once she felt happy and airy and free,

the light had done something quite special indeed.

She cradled that sparkle and ran to her den,

she found an old jar to put the light in—

now for the stew—she thought, I'll add just a fleck,

of this wonderful, giddy, lively light speck.

And as she turned to take a bit from the jar,

she noticed the speck had turned into a star!

It got bigger and brighter and then don't cha know...

It said—

"I must get out—I have places to go!

For I am the mother of the twinkles you see—

in the eyes of the children—yes, that is me!

That feeling you got as you cupped me within,

is what I share with those whose twinkles gone dim.

The wonderful oldsters who've gone a bit blind

'cause they lost their twinkles-so their twinkles, I find.

They have stories to tell and tickles that place

smiles and grins on each youngster's face!

My job is immense and I must get back to it

and you've made it impossible for me to go do it!

I'll keep getting larger and this jar won't hold...

Unfortunately, soon I will simply explode.

And then I'll be gone and there never will be

twinkling eyes of some oldsters you see... but

since your hands have held me, my spirit now knows,

if I fail at the job-to you she will go."

The old witch thought, Ahhhh, that power could be mine.

The things I could do with this wee jar of shine.

And she pondered the thought... Oh yes, it'd be grand-

to be the twinkle mother of all the land!

So, she ignored the light in the jar that got brighter,

And her den became lighter and lighter and lighter.

Then, it happened, oh yes, a low distant roar.

The roll of thunder, came to her door.

Then the jar exploded, darkness filled the room.

the twinkling spark had escaped with a boom!

She felt herself rising and as she looked down—

she saw all of the people of her little ol' town.

Then, she saw the city that loomed to the east,

and then she saw the continents lying beneath.

Her eyesight sharpened and she took in the sights.

Her name became Twinkle Witch on that very night.

Now, her job is immense and her days are forever.

You see, she had taken on quite an endeavor.

And she's having some trouble—she could use a hand,

from all of you children—so, here is the plan.

You must keep track of your twinkle, you see,

that'll make the Twinkle Witch quite happy.

'Cause then when you get old, we all do ya know—

she won't get an e-mail that says she must go

find your special twinkle that you somehow lost—

'cause you can't buy a new twinkle at any cost.

Your twinkle is yours—no one else's, you see—

can have the same twinkle as you or as me.

And believe me, you'll need that spark in your eye,

to tell your grandchildren about the witch of the sky

and how she finds twinkles and puts them back in

the eyes of those oldsters whose eyesight's gone dim.

Because they lost their twinkle somehow, somewhere,

between their teens and impending gray hair.

All you dear children can you say with me now...

This simple promise... this solemn vow?

Oh, Witch of the Sky (Oh, Witch of the Sky)

I promise I'll try (I promise I'll try)

To keep my Twinkle (To keep my twinkle)

In my eye (In my eye)

Now, off with you children-go skitter about.

Or lay your head down if it's time for lights out.

Tend to your twinkle—keep it shiny and bright.

So ye ol' Twinkle Witch can see you each night.

And in years to come she won't get that e-mail,

requesting her help finding your twinkle's trail.

THE
END

Lightning Source UK Ltd.
Milton Keynes UK
UKHW050646080921
389946UK00008B/23